LEN ALLOCCO

Lily & Josie Find A Friend

To order additional copies of this book, contact:
Xlibris
844-714-8691
www.Xlibris.com
Orders@Xlibris.com

ISBN: 978-1-6698-5513-2 (sc)
ISBN: 978-1-6698-5514-9 (e)

Print information available on the last page

Rev. date: 11/11/2022

Lily & Josie
Find A Friend

Lily is the oldest,
she likes to ride her bike;
Josie is the youngest,
She follows on her trike.

They peddle up the driveway,
and down the sidewalk path,
They ride their way to Jamie's house,
and round the stone bird bath.

Jamie is their neighbor,
she's almost eight years old.
She likes to laugh and play with them,
and brush her hair of gold.

When Jamie saw the two girls
approaching and she said;
"Come look and see what I discovered
in our garden bed!"

9

So Lily and her sister,
got off their bikes and ran;
to where the garden flowers grew,
next to the tan sedan.

12

And there upon the parsley leaves,
a caterpillar sat;
his lime green belly stretched an inch
with black stripes on his back.

So Lily said to Josie,
"Let's get a jelly jar.
We'll put him in with parsley leaves
so he won't roam too far."

They found out he's a larva,
who's future will be bright;
but first he must cocoon himself,
and grow two wings for flight.

One morning when the girls woke up,
they saw a green cocoon;
"He's in there and he's fast asleep;
we'll look again at noon."

He's called a Pupa Jamie said,
"A crystallis is inside";
and Josie said with wonderment,
"So that's why he muat hide."

Each day they looked to see if he,
became a butterfly.
But nothing changed; he looked the same
and many days went by.

But then one day to their surprise,
a butterfly appeared!
With black wings and some color dots;
the girls jumped up and cheered!

They showed it to their mother,
who was drinking ginger ale;
And she said,"Glory-oskie girls;
You've got a Swallowtail!"

They took the clean clear jelly jar,
outside where he could fly;
and as he climbed out carefully,
he waived and said "Goodbye"

At summer's end when school began,
the girls were Shining Stars!
With larva, pupa, and parsley leaves...

in clear clean jelly jars!

Printed in the United States
by Baker & Taylor Publisher Services